# SHORTSTOP FROM TOKYO

# Books by Matt Christopher

# SHORTSTOP
## FROM
# TOKYO

*by Matt Christopher*

Illustrated by Harvey Kidder

*Little, Brown and Company*
**Boston · Toronto · London**

LIBRARY OF CONGRESS CATALOG CARD NO. 72—97141

FIRST PAPERBACK EDITION

ISBN 0-316-13992-0

10   9   8   7   6   5   4

VB

*Published simultaneously in Canada*
*by Little, Brown & Company (Canada) Limited*

PRINTED IN THE UNITED STATES OF AMERICA

*to*
Joe, Jan, Chandra, Kihm and Joey

# 1

"GET two, Stogie!"

"Let 'er come!" Stogie Crane yelled, back-trotting to deep short. He smacked the pocket of his glove a couple of times and crouched forward, arms dangling, at the edge of the infield grass.

Coach Bob Dirkus, standing by home plate, tossed up the ball and rapped a hot, bouncing grounder a few feet to Stogie's right side. The wiry shortstop rushed behind it, fielded the ball neatly, and whipped it underhand to second. Second baseman Russ Russo caught it on the bag

3

and pegged it to first. The peg was high but Bob Sobus jumped and speared it.

"Home it!" yelled the coach.

Bob, a left-hander, pivoted on his left foot and whipped the ball to Tony Francis. Tony pegged it across the diamond to Stogie, covering the keystone sack. His throw was high too, and Stogie had to jump. He snared the ball in the small web of his glove, laughed over it, then pegged it to Fuzzy Caliel at third and Fuzzy winged it home.

"Two again!" yelled the coach.

Stogie Crane smiled across at Russ. "Muff it and you're a hunk of cheese!"

"You're on!" cried Russ.

The grounder was to Russ's left side. He got behind it, nabbed it and fired it to second. Stogie, grinning like a cat, caught it at his knees on the run, stepped on the

4

sack and whipped it to first. It was a strike throw. Bob caught it and zipped it back to Russ, who had to run hard to cover his base. The throw was wide and sailed out to the outfield, where an outfielder picked it up and tossed it in.

"What do you want me to do — throw it into your pocket?" yelled Bob.

The skinny second baseman wiped his brow and flicked the sweat off his fingers. "I'm sorry. I left my long arms home!"

Stogie chuckled. "Just make those throws good when we tackle the Copperheads," he reminded.

"Snakes alive!" cried Russ. "We playing those guys tomorrow?"

"Playing, you say? Man, you'd better not forget your tommy-hawks! We'd better slaughter those guys in the first inning. We can't —"

"Quit your jabbering out there and get down to business!" yelled Coach Dirkus. "Get two, Bob!"

Bob caught the big hop, rifled it home, caught Tony's quick return throw on the bag, then pegged the ball across the diamond to Fuzzy.

"Hey, Stogie," said Russ, as Fuzzy lollied the ball in to home. "Here comes what's-his-name, that Japanese kid."

"Sam Suzuki," said Stogie.

The kid had just come around the dugout with a short, stoutish man who was his father. Sam Suzuki was short, too, for his age. He was about as old as Stogie and the other kids on the Mohawk baseball team. What surprised Stogie was that Sam was wearing a Mohawk uniform. Boy, he certainly hadn't wasted time in getting acquainted with Coach Dirkus. Well, maybe the coach wanted no argument with Sam's father, a judo expert.

The coach waved to Mr. Suzuki, then motioned Sam forward. Sam, carrying a glove, smiled and ran up to him. Stogie couldn't hear what they said, but in a moment he could guess. Sam pointed toward short and then came running out.

"That's Sam Suzuki, Stogie!" Coach Dirkus yelled. "Introduce yourself! Then I want you to alternate with him!"

Stogie's chin dropped. He forced a smile to try to match the one plastered over Sam's face and stuck out his hand. "Hi, Sam. I'm Stogie Crane."

"Hi, Stogie. I am Hideko Suzuki. Call me Sam."

Stogie's smile faded slightly. "Did you play shortstop in Japan?"

"I always play shortstop. My favorite

position." Sam laughed. "You are not worried I play shortstop too, I hope?"

"No." But Stogie's smile flickered, then died.

Heck, why should he be worried? Sam didn't really expect to take over the shortstop position, did he? Besides, Coach Dirkus seldom let a kid play a full game. He would put in a sub about the fourth or fifth inning.

"Heads up, Russ!" cried the coach.

He bunted the ball in front of the plate. Tony flung off his mask, scurried across the plate, scooped up the ball and pegged it to second. Russ caught it, snapped it to first, and Bob whipped it back to home.

"All right, now! Get one!"

Fuzzy fielded the low hopper and made the throw to first. The ball sailed home, back to Bob, then home again.

"Stogie!"

Stogie set himself at the edge of the grass, snatched the grass-cutting grounder, and pegged it letter-high to Bob. Sam's turn was next. Stogie backed him up, smiling as he watched the coach hit a soft grounder to the Japanese boy. Sam charged the ball, caught it near the ground, snapped it underhand to Bob, then hustled to cover second.

Bob whipped the ball to him. Sam nabbed it out of the air, spun, and pegged it to third. The ball traveled like a white bullet.

"Nice going, Sam!" yelled Coach Dirkus.

Sam looked around and smiled at Stogie. "How do I look?" asked Sam proudly.

"Good, Sam," said Stogie. "You look good."

# 2

"RUSSO! Peters! Crane! Let's start off with some bingles!"

It was the next day and the Mohawks' third game of the season. Coach Bob Dirkus stood in the sun next to the dugout, holding a pad. He wore regular pants, but his shirt was part of a baseball uniform he used to wear when he had played with the Westport Eagles. His black cap, the letter M on it, was the same as the Mohawk players'.

Larry Hill, the Copperheads' tall left-hander, finished throwing his warm-up pitches and Russ stepped to the plate.

"Look at 'im hug the plate," observed Fuzzy. "It's a wonder he doesn't put his arms around it."

"That's his strategy," said Dennis Krupa, a sub infielder. "Ten to one he gets on."

Larry Hill fired two balls outside of the plate, got one over, then another for a two-and-two count. Russ stepped out of the box and rubbed his hands in the soft dirt.

"His hands get hot quickly," said Sam Suzuki, laughing. "Maybe should carry towel. Not so dirty."

Stogie, standing to the right of the dugout with his bat, heard it all. The guys laughed, but he couldn't see anything at all funny in the remark.

*Crack!* Russ belted a one-hopper to third. The Copperhead third baseman snagged it easily and whipped it to first. "Out!" yelled the base umpire.

Beak Peters stepped into the box next. He was built like a young tree and had a nose that seemed to be too big for his face.

He let two pitches go by, both strikes, then stepped back and jiggled his helmet a couple of times. He walked back into the box and blasted the next pitch through the pitcher's box, making Larry Hill jump like a scared cat.

"Your man, Stogie!" Fuzzy yelled. "Let's start a merry-go-round!"

Stogie looked at Coach Dirkus. "If it's in there, belt it," said the coach.

The Copperhead infielders were talking it up, sounding like ten men out there instead of four. The Copperhead catcher was talking it up too, sounding like a stuck needle on a phonograph. "Right in here, Larry! Right in here, boy! Right in here, Larry! Right in here, boy!"

*Boom!* Stogie's bat connected with the ball and sent it cruising through space toward left center field. Beak streaked to second, rounded third, and bolted for home as the third base coach windmilled him on. The left fielder finally got the ball and pegged it in to third, forcing Stogie back to second for a neat double.

Stogie looked across the diamond at Sam Suzuki and saw the Japanese boy clapping thunderously. Somehow Stogie felt he needed that hit. He wanted to show Coach Dirkus he was still the best man to play shortstop.

Jim Albanese, up next, popped the first pitch to short for out number two.

Bob Sobus came up. A left-handed hitter, he stood at the plate straight as an arrow, his legs spread apart just a little, his bat held inches off his left shoulder.

Larry Hill slipped a strike past him. Bob swung at the next pitch and missed it for strike two. He swung at the third, and this time bat met ball and sent it hopping like a frightened rabbit between first and second. Stogie rounded third and scored. The throw-in held Bob at first.

"All right, Fuzzy-wuzzy," said Dennis. "Practice what you preach."

"Got your movie camera?" asked Fuzzy. "I'd like to do a commercial first."

"Get up there and hit!" Coach Dirkus hollered at him.

Larry Hill stretched and delivered. The throw went into the dirt and past the catcher's mitt to the backstop screen. Bob Sobus trotted to second.

"Three more like that and you'll have it made, Fuzzy!" yelled Beak.

Larry Hill didn't throw three more like that. He sizzled two over the plate, then one up around Fuzzy's neck which Fuzzy swung at and missed. "Strike three!"

"Guess you should've done a commercial anyhow," said Stogie, running out with him. "You might've made a hit."

Fuzzy laughed. "Wasn't my fault there wasn't a camera around!"

Stretch Servo, the Mohawk pitcher, walked the Copperhead lead-off hitter. The next batter hit a clothesline drive to Stogie. One out. Stogie whipped it to first and picked off the runner before he could tag up. Two outs! The third Copperhead took two strikes in a row, then lined a drive between right and center for two bases. The next batter singled, driving him

16

in. Stretch mowed the fifth batter down with three pitched strikes.

"Start it off, Bernie," said the coach at the top of the second inning.

Right fielder Bernie Drake did — with a pop-up. Tony Francis singled, then Stretch went down swinging. Lead-off man Russ Russo took two called strikes, then laced a single through short. Tony galloped around second and held up at third.

"Knock him in, Beak!" yelled Fuzzy. "Don't let 'im die there!"

Beak fanned.

The Copperheads picked up two runs, one of them on an error by Fuzzy. Stogie, leading off in the top of the third, took a hard-swinging cut at the first pitch and belted it a mile. Only it was straight up. It came down from its dizzying height and the Copperhead third baseman caught it.

"Too bad," said Sam. "Should be that way." He pointed toward left field.

"I know," said Stogie, squeezing between a couple of guys on the bench. *I wonder if Coach Dirkus figures on playing Sam,* he thought.

Jim Albanese doubled. Bob Sobus walked. Then Fuzzy Caliel swung all the way around on a slow pitch — swung hard enough to drive the ball into the next state. But the little white apple did nothing but dribble down toward third. Fuzzy dropped his bat and scampered for first as if a ghost were after him, and made it. The cheers that exploded from the fans were the loudest Fuzzy had received so far this year.

18

"Bases loaded!" yelled Beak. "Clean 'em, Bernie! You're due, man!"

Bernie tripled.

"There ya go!" cried Beak, clapping furiously.

Tony struck out and Stretch flied out to finish the big three-run inning.

Stretch retired the first Copperhead on five pitches, then walked the next one. Stogie came in slightly and moved a few steps closer to second as a left-hand batter strode to the plate. The lefty blasted a long high fly to center which sent Beak Peters back a dozen steps. He caught the ball and pegged it in, holding the runner on first.

The next hitter uncorked a drive that went looping over Stogie's head. Stogie ran back sideways, gloved hand stretched out, his eyes on the ball that seemed to be floating through the air like a balloon. It skimmed his glove and struck the grass. He caught the bounce, looked back, and saw the runner arriving at second base. No play. He relayed the ball to Fuzzy, who carried it halfway to Stretch before tossing it to him.

The next batter hit a high grounder to Fuzzy, who touched third for a force-out. Three away.

Mohawks 5, Copperheads 3. The top of the fourth coming up.

"Stogie, I want Sam to hit for you," said the coach. "Ready, Sammy?"

Sam beamed. "Ready all the time," he said happily.

# 3

RUSS RUSSO led off in the top of the fourth with a looping single over second. The coach signaled Lee Cragg (pinch-hitting for Beak) to bunt, but Lee's first two tries resulted in fouls. He had to swing now. He took two balls, then lashed hard at the next pitch, sending it high into the air over short. The Copperhead shortstop grabbed it for the first out.

"Okay, Sam," said Fuzzy. "Show 'em how you do it in Tokyo."

"Tokyo?" Tony Francis frowned. "Is that where he's from?"

"Sure. Where did you think he's from —
Mexico City?"

Sam whipped a couple of bats around
a few times, then dropped one and stepped
to the plate.

"He spreads his legs awful wide for a
short guy," observed Dennis.

"And look at him wave that bat around,"
said Fuzzy. "Maybe he's chasing the bugs
away."

*Smack!* Sam Suzuki connected with the
first pitch. The ball sailed over the third
baseman's head, curved outward, and
struck the ground just inside the foul line.
The entire Mohawk bench stood on their
feet. "Go! Go!"

By the time the left fielder had relayed
the ball in, Russ had scored and Sam was
perched nicely on third base.

"A triple!" cried Fuzzy, clapping thun-

derously. "How 'bout that? And the first pitch, too!" He laughed at Stogie. "Looks like you've just lost your job, Stogie, ol' boy!"

Stogie grinned politely. He tried hard to hide a feeling that had been gnawing at him ever since Sam Suzuki had come upon the scene. That triple had magnified the feeling a hundred times over. Yet it was strange. He didn't know exactly what that feeling was. Was it envy? Was it jealousy? Maybe it was one or the other, or both. But he knew it wasn't right to be envious or jealous of anyone. Envy and jealousy destroyed friendship, and made you feel sick inside, too.

Jim Albanese popped up to the catcher for the second out. Bob Sobus took a strike, then pitcher Larry Hill lost his control and walked him. Dennis Krupa batted for

Fuzzy and grounded out to end the half inning.

"If I knew you were going to do that," grumbled Fuzzy, "I would've batted myself." As if he had anything to say about it.

The Mohawks trotted out to their positions and the Copperheads came to bat.

Coach Dirkus squeezed in between Stogie and Fuzzy on the bench. "Sam tell you guys about that glove of his?" he asked, grinning.

"Not me," said Stogie.

"Me, either," said Fuzzy. The other guys edged closer.

"He's really proud of it, you know," said the coach. "It seems a famous Japanese ball player, Shigeo Nagashima, signed his name on the glove. So it's worth a lot to Sam."

Russ fumbled a grounder, putting a

man on first. The next hitter clobbered a long high fly that went clean over the left field fence for a homer. Stretch looked nervous on the mound after that, even though the infielders and outfielders chattered to cheer him up.

A grounder sizzled like a scared snake down to short. Stogie watched intently as Sam crouched, waiting for it. *Miss it! Miss it!* Stogie couldn't help wishing silently.

Sam caught the wild grounder and pegged it to first. His throw was like a tight string drawn across the diamond, incredible for a little guy.

"Look at that arm!" exclaimed Coach Dirkus. "The kid can really throw!"

Stretch chalked up a strikeout. Another hot grounder to Sam, which he caught easily and pegged to first for an out, ended

the half inning. The scoreboard at the left
of the left field foul line read:

| Innings | 1 | 2 | 3 | 4 | 5 | 6 |
|---------|---|---|---|---|---|---|
| MOHAWKS | 2 | 0 | 3 | 1 |   |   |
| C HEADS | 1 | 2 | 0 | 2 |   |   |

Daren Holden singled for Bernie Drake
in the top of the fifth. Tony Francis followed with another single. Then Stretch
came through with a double, scoring
Daren and advancing Tony to third. Russ
popped up to the pitcher. Then Lee Cragg
blasted a line drive to short and the shortstop picked off Stretch at second before he
could tag up. Three away.

The Copperheads picked up a run in the
bottom of the fifth. But the Mohawks,
even though Sam Suzuki got his second
hit of the game, a double, couldn't score.

The Copperheads, at bat for their last chance, failed to hit. One of their outs was a pop fly on the grass far behind Sam. He ran back and caught the ball on the fingertips of his glove, drawing a tremendous cheer from the crowd. Mohawks 7, Copperheads 6.

"Sam certainly played a wonderful ball game," said Jill, Stogie's older sister. "I didn't know they played baseball in Japan."

"Huh!" Stogie snorted. "They probably play more baseball than we do. They draw bigger crowds, that's for sure. Haven't you ever heard about our big league teams going over there and playing their teams?"

"When I read the sports pages I read about our girls' softball team, not about big league teams playing in Japan," said Jill haughtily.

Dad chuckled. He and Mom were walking behind Stogie, Jill, Beak and Fuzzy. "Tell you one thing about Sam Suzuki," he said. "He's an all-around baseball player. He can hit, throw and field like nobody's business. And being among strangers his first day didn't seem to bother him a bit."

Fuzzy laughed. "Bother him? I guess not! I've never seen a kid like him in my life!"

An hour later someone knocked on the back door. Jill answered it. "Stogie!" she called. "It's Beak and Sam."

Beak and *Sam?* Stogie went to the door. "Hi," he said, not too enthusiastically. Then he saw their gloves. Play baseball again? They'd just finished a game!

"Hi!" greeted Sam, smacking the pocket

of his glove with a small fist. "Like to play pepper?"

Beak grinned. "He came over to my house and asked if I'd come here so's the three of us can play hit and catch," said Beak. "I told him we called it 'pepper.'"

Stogie thought about it a minute. He really wasn't keen about playing pepper. He'd been reading a sports book and was at an interesting section. But since Sam had asked Beak to come over, Stogie knew he should be decent to him.

"Okay," he said. "I'll get my bat."

Sam's face lit up like a lamp. "Good!" he exclaimed happily.

Stogie got his bat and they played in the backyard. The boys stood with their backs to the woods behind them. The woods extended high up into the hills, the northern border of Westport. The city was small, but had a college attended by students from all over the world. Surrounding the city were the woods, and every once in a while a deer, a raccoon, a porcupine, or some other wild animal would be seen roaming a street, though never was one of them caught.

"What does your father do?" Stogie asked as he knocked a slow grounder down to Sam.

"He is a professor at Westport College," replied Sam. "He won a fellowship from the university in Tokyo."

"Then you're not going to be in the United States very long?" Stogie asked almost hopefully.

"One year."

"You speak pretty good English," remarked Beak. "Been taking it in school?"

"Oh, sure! Been in United States one

year before, too. I want to talk English very well."

Sam's next pitch was too far inside. Stogie jumped back and swung, striking the underside of the ball. It popped high and at an angle behind him. He spun and saw it head straight for a side window of the house next door. The Bunningers! Two people who hated the sight of baseballs, footballs, bowling balls, or anything else that was round and connected with sports!

*Smash!* The ball sailed through the window, shattering it to pieces.

Stogie stood frozen on the spot.

# 4

THE BACK DOOR of the Bunninger house swung open as if a strong wind had blown it. A tall man in shirt sleeves and baggy pants burst out on the porch, his red face matching his glaring eyes.

"Scalawagging devils!" he shouted, the white strands of hair on his shiny scalp standing almost straight up. "Know what you've done? You didn't only break that window! You smashed a vase too! A vase over a hundred years old!"

"S-s-s-sorry, M-Mr. B-Bunninger!" stammered Stogie.

"Sorry?" Mr. Bunninger waggled like a duck down the steps, holding the baseball in his hand. "That doesn't pay for a window! That doesn't pay for a vase Mrs. Bunninger's grandmother left her! Darn scalawagging . . . ! You know what oughta be done with every baseball in these here United States? Put into a big cannon and shot at those Communists, that's what! Whoever invented the dang game oughta be tied to a stake and burned!"

"It's too late," said Beak softly. "He's dead."

Mr. Bunninger stopped at the fence and stared at him. "Who's dead?"

"Abner Doubleday," answered Beak. "He's the guy who invented baseball."

"Oh? You even know the guy who invented the game, do you?" Mr. Bunninger's voice rasped as if his vocal chords were lined with sandpaper. "Well, that don't cut no ice! Somebody's still carrying on his lousy tradition! Baseball! This is proof, ain't it? This is proof it's a dangerous sport! Just like football, basketball, soccer and the whole shootin' match of 'em! No wonder this country's goin' to the dogs!"

Suddenly he looked directly at Sam Suzuki. The flames in his eyes died a little. "Who are you? Never seen you before."

"Sam Suzuki." Sam, who had looked pretty frightened throughout Mr. Bunninger's long speech, cracked a weak smile.

"Sam Suzuki? Live in Westport?"

Sam's head bobbed.

"Since when?"

"Since two weeks ago. My father is a professor at the college."

"Oh. Where did you come from? China? Japan? Korea?"

Sam chuckled. "Tokyo, Japan."

A smile smothered the flames altogether in Mr. Bunninger's eyes. "Tokyo, huh? Always wanted to visit Tokyo. Beautiful city. Big, loaded with temptations."

The boys stared at him. Sam hauled out his Japanese-American pocket dictionary. "Tem what?" he asked.

Mr. Bunninger laughed. "Forget it." Then his eyes went back to the baseball in his hand and he stopped laughing. His sandpapery voice became serious again. "I'll tell you a secret if you promise you won't spill it to my wife. Promise?"

Sam returned the dictionary to his pocket, obviously disappointed that Mr.

Bunninger had refused to repeat the word.

"Promise," said Stogie.

"You'll have to pay for the window," said Mr. Bunninger sharply. "Might be five bucks. I don't know. Maybe less, maybe more. The vase — now, that's different. This is the secret I want you to keep. Spill it to Mrs. Bunninger and I'll keep after you three till I track you down and tan your backsides till they're blistered." He leaned forward and lowered his voice. *"I'm glad the accident happened,* hear? That vase was the ugliest piece of furniture we had in the house. I've been trying to think of ways to get rid of it ever since we've been married. Point is, she admitted it wasn't the prettiest object of art in the world, herself, but she wouldn't get rid of it because it was a family heirloom."

40

Stogie sucked in a deep breath and let it out. "But what're you going to tell your wife when she sees the broken vase, Mr. Bunninger?"

"Tell her the truth. What else? Sure, she'll be mad. But I'll tell her I bawled you out good and proper. And I did, didn't I?"

"You sure did!" said Sam elatedly.

Mr. Bunninger's eyes hopped from one boy to the other like Ping-Pong balls. The fierceness had returned to them. Without saying another word, he pivoted and started back towards his house.

"Mr. Bunninger," Stogie called. "You still have our baseball."

The old man paused, looked at the ball, then tossed it across the fence. "Can't see what fun you kids get out of baseball. Can't see it at all. Don't forget that win-

41

dow. I'll get it fixed and give you the bill."

"Yes, sir," promised Stogie.

After Mr. Bunninger disappeared into the house Stogie looked at Sam. "I'll pay for it," he said.

"No. Me. I will pay for the window. I threw the ball wide. It was my mistake."

"But I hit it," argued Stogie. "I should pay for it."

"Tell you what," intervened Beak. "The three of us will pay for it. We were all playing so we should all pay."

Sam and Stogie looked at each other. Sam grinned and Stogie shrugged. "It's settled," announced Beak.

Jill appeared at the door, carrying a tray with three tall glasses on it. "Lemonade, anyone?"

"It's funny," said Beak. "I was just hoping someone would come and say, 'Lemonade, anyone?' "

They sat on the lawn and drank and talked about the Bunningers. Then Sam told about his life in Japan and about the Yomiuri Giants, his favorite baseball team, and about Shigeo Nagashima, the Giants' great home run hitter whose autograph Sam had on his glove. He had learned judo, too, as his father had. And he could eat with chopsticks, but the family had been eating with knives and forks for so long that they preferred to continue eating that way. Television? His favorite actor was John Wayne.

The sound of two loud blasts and a short one ended their talk abruptly. A couple of seconds later the blasts were repeated.

Sam sprang to his feet. "What's that?"

"A fire!"

Moments later they heard a fire truck roaring up a nearby street, its bell clanging.

"Let's see where it is!" cried Beak.

Stogie practically dropped the tray with the empty glasses on the porch and ran out of the yard behind Beak and Sam. The fire was two blocks away. Smoke and flames were leaping from the second story windows of a house and firemen were shooting water through them from hoses. Police were keeping the crowd back and detouring cars down another street.

Half an hour later some of the firemen had entered the building and the fire was pretty much under control. But darkness had fallen and suddenly Beak said, "Hey!

I'd better get home. My folks will wonder where I am."

"My folks, too," said Sam. "Come on!"

The three of them raced down to the corner, then cut sharply onto Huckleberry Street.

"Good night, Stogie!" cried Beak as Stogie headed toward the rear of his house.

" 'Night! 'Night, Sam!"

"Good night, Stogie! See you tomorrow!"

Stogie started for the back porch when he saw a glove on the lawn. He recognized it immediately as Sam Suzuki's. He looked for Beak's, then remembered that Beak had strapped his to his belt.

Stogie picked up the glove and saw Shigeo Nagashima's autograph on it. I ought to take it to Sam, he thought. He'll wonder what happened to it.

Then he remembered Sam's playing shortstop, remembered the coach's praising him. "Look at that arm! The kid can really throw!"

Resentment burst within him and he chucked the glove back onto the lawn. *The heck with the darn glove,* he told himself. *Sam forgot it. Let him take care of it himself.*

He climbed the steps and went into the house.

# 5

SAM CAME over for the glove in the morning. His face shone radiantly as the sun. "Forgot glove," he said. "You take it into the house?"

Stogie looked past Sam's shoulder. "No. It's on the lawn. I saw it there last night."

"Not on the lawn," said Sam. "I look."

Stogie frowned. He focused his eyes on the spot where he clearly remembered having seen Sam's glove. It wasn't there. "Funny," he said and ran down the steps.

"You sure you did not take it into the

house?" asked Sam, his own forehead creased from puzzlement now.

"I told you I didn't," insisted Stogie, his voice rising sharply. Where was that lousy glove anyway? It was here last night. No one would've come here after dark and taken it. No one except Sam and Stogie had known it was here. And probably Beak. But why should Beak worry about Sam Suzuki's glove? He had his own to think about, and he had taken it with him.

Suddenly a yell tore from Sam. "I see it!"

He dashed toward the far side of the lawn and Stogie breathed a sigh of relief. But how did the glove get over there?

Sam picked it up. Then he stood, staring at it in horror.

"What's the matter, Sam?" yelled Stogie, running forward. "It's yours, isn't it?"

And then he stopped and stared, too. The inside of the glove was torn to ribbons and most of the packing was sticking out.

Sam looked at Stogie, tears springing to his eyes.

"You did this!" he exclaimed, his lips trembling.

"Me? Are you crazy?"

"You do not want me to play shortstop!" cried Sam. "You were mad and destroyed my glove! Autograph of Shigeo Nagashima destroyed too!" Sam's voice cracked. He folded the glove and ran out of the yard as fast as he could.

Stogie ran after him. "Sam!" he yelled. "Sam! I didn't destroy your glove! I didn't!"

Sam fled around the corner of the house and out of sight. A lump filled Stogie's throat. He hadn't destroyed Sam's glove! But someone had.

"What was that all about?" a voice inquired. Stogie looked up and saw Jill and Mom staring at him from the top of the porch steps.

"Some — someone's ruined Sam Suzuki's glove," he murmured, "and he blames me. I didn't do it, but he won't believe me."

"Did he have it with him?" Mom asked, frowning.

"No. He left it here last night." Stogie felt a sense of guilt. "We'd gone to a fire — Sam, Beak and me — and Sam left his glove. He went home afterwards instead of coming back here after it. I — I saw it lying on the lawn, but I — I just left it. That's all. I just left it. I — I never thought anything might happen to it."

"Maybe a dog got after it," Jill guessed.

"I don't know," said Stogie, climbing slowly up the steps. "But Sam believes I did it. He thinks I'm jealous of him, that I'm afraid he'll take over shortstop."

"That's silly," exclaimed Jill. "Sam wouldn't think that."

"Oh, no? Try telling Sam that. See if he doesn't."

Beak came over later and Stogie told him about the glove.

"That's right!" said Beak, his eyes flashing wide. "He didn't take the glove with him when we went to the fire! I remember! I could kick myself for not reminding him about it when we came back."

"I could kick myself for leaving it on the lawn," muttered Stogie. "I picked it up . . . to take to him. Then I left it there on purpose."

"Why?" Beak frowned at him.

A ball clogged in Stogie's throat. "Because, that's why! Quit asking me silly questions, will you?"

# 6

STOGIE CRANE was at the ball field at six o'clock. A few minutes later Sam arrived with Bernie Drake and Jim Albanese. Sam had his glove. *It's ruined inside but he still wants to use it,* Stogie thought. *Gosh, it would be like catching a ball with your bare hand!*

He wanted to catch Sam's eyes, to say "Hi" or something. But Sam was busy playing catch with Bernie and Jim. Now and then Stogie saw him wince as he caught a fast throw in the pocket of the glove. Sam didn't yell. And from his smil-

ing face you'd never know that deep inside
he was hurt.

The Patriots had first raps. Stogie, playing short for the Mohawks, joined the chatter with the other infielders — "C'mon,
Tom! Get 'im out, Tom, boy!" — shouting
Tom Rolf's name and hoping to blot out
the thought of Sam and his ruined glove.

A Patriot singled. The next slashed a
grounder down to short. The ball came
directly at Stogie. He crouched, waiting
for the hop. The ball struck the heel of his
glove, bounced up against his chest and
then to the ground. Panic-stricken, he re-
trieved the ball, started to throw to second, but held up.

Whoops! The ball slipped out of his
hand! Panic flared in him again as he
pounced after it, picked it up, looked
around quickly. The runners were holding

their bases, one on first, the other on second.

"That's all right, Stogie!" yelled Fuzzy Caliel. "Let's keep 'em from getting to third!"

Tom Rolf threw two balls, then cut the heart of the plate for a strike. The next was nearly in the same spot and the Patriot connected with it solidly. The ball traveled on a tightrope between center and left, scoring one run, and leaving a runner on third and the batter on second for a clean double.

Tom hit the next Patriot to load the bases. Beak Peters caught a long fly in deep center field and pegged the ball in, but not quickly enough to stop another run from scoring. A second double scored two more runs, which was all the Patriots got that top of the first inning. It was a lot.

"Let's get 'em back, Russ!" yelled Coach Dirkus. "Hit it when it's in there!"

Whitey Beach, the Patriots' right-handed hurler, had trouble putting a strike over. Russ walked. Beak hit a scratch single to short, beating out the shortstop's throw. Russ made second easily. Then Stogie was up, sweat clinging to his brow, more from nervousness than from running and the summer heat.

He slashed at the first pitch and missed it. "Strike!" yelled the ump.

He ticked the next pitch. "Strike two!"

His heart pounded furiously as the third pitch came in. It was high, but he had already started to swing and couldn't stop now. He missed the ball by six inches.

"Strike three!"

"C'mon, Stoge!" cried Bob Sobus cheerlessly. "That pitch was a mile high!"

Jim Albanese grounded out and Bob flied out to end the half inning. In the top of the next, the Mohawks held the Patriots scoreless, then picked up two runs in their half of the second to make the score 4 to 2.

In the top of the third the first Patriot lined a smashing drive down to Stogie. Stogie's heart shot to his throat as he waited for it. His nerves were tight and he expected to muff the ball. He did! The ball struck the thumb of his glove, glanced against his right leg and skittered behind him. He fell backward as he tried to spin on his heel, then got up and started after the ball. But Fuzzy was picking it up.

"Got troubles, Stoge?" he asked with a deadpan face.

"You can say that again," replied Stogie. "But don't."

Tom wiped out the next hitter with a strikeout. The next Patriot flied out to first. A clean single advanced the runner to third, but Tom worked hard on the next man and the Patriot popped up to Tony Francis.

The Mohawks picked up a run at their turn at bat. Then the Patriots got on to Tom for two runs in the fourth and three in the fifth, while the Mohawks scored only once in each of those innings. Sam had taken Stogie's place in the top of the fourth, belting out a single. In the bottom of the sixth he knocked out a double, the only player to hit that inning, to give himself two for two in the three innings he had played.

The Patriots won, 9 to 5. And Stogie feared he was going to lose his starting position at short to Sam Suzuki for sure.

# 7

THE BUNNINGERS had a new window installed the following day. Stogie went over and paid for the bill out of his allowance and later got a third of the cost from Beak.

"Sam pay you yet?" asked Beak.

"No. And I won't ask him," replied Stogie.

"Why not? He said he'd pay his share."

"I know he did. But I'm not going to ask him for it. For crying out loud, Beak, I told you! I feel responsible for what happened to his glove. I can't ask him to pay for his share of the window."

"Okay. I know how you feel, Stoge. Guess I'd feel the same way if I were in your shoes."

Stogie was in for a surprise when he arrived at the field that evening with Beak and Jim Albanese. "I want you to play second base today, Stogie," advised the coach. "I've an idea that you and Sam will make a terrific combination round the keystone sack."

Stogie's cheeks puffed up like a bun. How do you like that? It had happened, just as he knew it would. Sam Suzuki had taken over short.

Hurt flickered in his eyes as he stared at the coach. "That's not fair, Coach!" he cried. "I'm the regular shortstop! Why don't you put Sam on second?"

The coach stared back at him. "Because I'm asking you to play there, Stogie," he answered firmly.

"But he's new. And I've been on the team —"

"He's always played shortstop, Stogie," Coach Dirkus interrupted quietly. "He loves it there."

"But I do, too!"

"It's different with you, Stogie. You're going to be with us a long time. Sam isn't. He might be here only a year. Maybe two. There's no harm in letting him play the position he knows best."

"I know shortstop best, too! I played only a little at second! When I started!"

It was hard fighting back the tears. Hard keeping that lump from crawling up to his throat.

"Well, you played a little, at least," replied Coach Dirkus. "You shouldn't have trouble adapting yourself to second."

"I'm not going to adapt myself to anything!" exploded Stogie. The words popped from his mouth without his even thinking. He blushed and stood riveted to the ground, staring at a blade of grass quivering in the wind.

"Okay, Stogie." Coach Dirkus took a deep breath and let it out. "Guess I have to remind you that my job isn't just making up lineups and knocking out grounders and flies. My job is to keep control of the team, too."

And then came the bomb.

"I think a little bench warming will do you good, Stogie."

Stogie's eyes widened. "What?"

"You heard me. You can sit for a while and remind yourself that what a coach

says goes, regardless of whether you like it or not. Dennis!" Coach Dirkus raised his voice sharply. "Take second!"

Dennis Krupa, the infield sub, looked in surprise from Stogie to the coach. "Okay, Coach," he said.

Stogie tightened his lips and held his breath for a dozen seconds. It wasn't fair. It just wasn't. Shortstop was his position. More grounders were hit there than to second. There were more right-hand batters, that was why. And that long throw from deep short to first base could only be matched by a throw from third. He loved to make those long throws. He could throw as hard as he wanted to, put all his steam in it, and then watch the ball speed across the diamond into the first baseman's mitt. No other position in the infield was more beautiful to him. That was what

Coach Dirkus had taken away from him and given to Sam Suzuki.

He noticed something on the field. Sam was playing catch with Fuzzy Caliel. Playing with a brand-new glove!

That meant that the old glove wasn't really good enough to play with. Stogie caught Sam's eyes a second and looked away. The old feeling came back.

*How can I change his mind and prove to him that I'm not all to blame for what happened to his glove?* he asked himself. *Sure, I could have taken it into the house, but how could I know something would get it and ruin it in our own backyard?* Man, what a lousy spot to be in!

The lineup today in the game against the Dukes was different in more ways than one.

Jim Albanese  lf
Lee Cragg   cf
Sam Suzuki   ss
Fuzzy Caliel  3b
Dennis Krupa   2b
Bob Sobus  1b
Daren Holden   rf
Tony Francis   c
Stretch Servo   p

As the Mohawks ran onto the field Sam stared across at Dennis, then at Stogie on the bench. Even from the bench Stogie could see the surprised look on Sam's face.

The chatter started in the Mohawk infield. It grew loudest at short. Sam Suzuki was a real live wire. You'd never guess he was so upset about his glove. No one would know. No one except him — and Stogie.

A smashing drive down to short! Sam caught the big hop, rifled it to first. Out!

"The old arm!" shouted Fuzzy as the ball zipped around the horn.

Crack! A reeling drive to second! Dennis moved to his left, bent forward, reached for the hop. Missed it! The ball rolled out to right field, where Daren Holden scooped it up and pegged it in.

*I would've had that,* reflected Stogie.

Stretch worked on the next hitter and got a three-two count on him. Then, smack! A hot grounder shooting between short and second! Sam bolted after it, caught it, snapped it to second. The ball struck the tips of Dennis's glove and bounced toward first. Both runners were safe.

Sam looked at Dennis, Dennis at Sam.

"My fault," Stogie heard Sam's apology.

Stretch was unable to throw a strike on the next batter and walked him.

"Bases crammed, Mike!" yelled a Duke fan. "Wipe it clean, boy!"

Mike almost did. He knocked a double, scoring two runs. Then a Duke popped out to first and another grounded out to third, ending the top of the first inning.

"You boys look a little nervous out there," observed the coach to Sam and Dennis. "Take it easy. Get behind the ball and make sure of your throws."

Jim walked and Lee Cragg advanced him to second on a sacrifice bunt. Sam Suzuki, up next, waved the bat around as if it were a toothpick. He took two strikes, then two balls, then laced a grounder down to third. The throw beat him by a step.

"Runs like a cat," said Bob Sobus.

Fuzzy walloped a straight-as-a-string liner over second for two bases, scoring

Jim. Dennis was up next. He took a called strike, then blasted a low pitch high over the infield. He was almost at first base when the Dukes' third baseman caught it. Three outs.

A slow bouncer to third earned a hit for the Dukes' lead-off batter. The next smashed a grounder to Dennis's left side. Dennis raced behind it, stuck out his glove and speared it. He spun on his heel and pegged it to second to get the double play.

A wild throw! Sam leaped off the bag after the ball. But instead of returning to it to get the runner out, he heaved the ball to first!

"Out!" yelled the base umpire.

The fans roared and screamed.

"Nice play, Sam," said Stretch.

Sam grinned. "Thank you," he said.

70

It was a nice play, Stogie had to admit. It was terrific. If he were in Sam's place he doubted that he would've thought to throw the ball to first. He would've tried for the putout on second base and would've failed. Sam wasn't only a player. He was a thinker too.

A triple scored the man on second, who would've been out if Dennis had made his double play throw good. That was all. The Mohawks came to bat trailing, 3 to 1.

# 8

BOB SOBUS took a called strike, then laced a high pitch to center field. The Duke caught it easily. Daren walked. Tony Francis, sweaty dirt streaking the sides of his face, punched a grounder to Toots Martin, the Duke pitcher. Toots snapped it to second. It went from there to first for a neat double play.

The Dukes' first batter socked a bouncing grounder to second. Stogie knew he could've caught it in his hip pocket. Dennis fielded it and threw the man out, getting a mixture of applause and laughter from the crowd.

A strikeout and a fly to left field retired the Dukes. Stretch, leading off for the Mohawks, laid into the first pitch and sent it bouncing between right and center for a double. Jim Albanese singled to score him. Then Lee Cragg flied out and Sam Suzuki, going after a low pitch on the third strike, struck out.

*Well!* thought Stogie. *Guess he misses 'em, too.*

Fuzzy Caliel banged the tip of his bat against the plate a couple of times, took a ball, then connected solidly with a letter-high pitch. The ball kept going . . . going . . . going . . .

It was a home run!

"Okay, Dennis! Keep the ol' ball rolling!"

Toots Martin had trouble getting a pitch over and Dennis won a free ticket to first. Bob Sobus, after fouling three straight pitches, popped up to Toots, ending the three-run rally. The Mohawks led, 4 to 3.

Top of the fourth. Stretch fanned the lead-off hitter, then got two strikes and three balls on the next. The Duke laced the sixth pitch down to Dennis's right side. Dennis charged after it, caught it, then turned to make the peg to first. His foot slipped and down he went.

"Tough luck, Den," said Stretch.

Jim muffed a fly ball in deep left field. By the time he relayed it in, runners were safely on second and third. The next Duke powdered a high pitch over short, scoring both runners. A pop fly was caught for the second out. Stretch walked the next man.

Then a hard single scored the Dukes' third run of the inning. Sam Suzuki's spearing catch of a line drive that seemed out of his reach for a second ended the Dukes' hot rally. Dukes 6, Mohawks 4.

"Some changes this inning," announced Coach Dirkus.

Stogie waited tensely. Would the coach forgive him and let him play now? Darn it, he didn't mean to pop off.

"Russ, bat for Daren. Beak, bat for Tony." His eyes passed over the members on the bench, including Stogie. That was it. No more changes. Stogie's heart sank.

Russ started off with a single. Then Beak singled, and Stogie, forgetting his troubles for a minute, grinned at his buddy standing with both feet firmly on first. Beak wanted to catch badly. But he just didn't have the arm that Tony had.

Stretch lambasted a pitch out to left. It was too high and not deep enough. The Duke outfielder made the catch easily. Jim Albanese, pulling on his helmet as he strode to the plate, got the long count, three and two, then smashed a liner over short. The hit went for two bases, scoring both Russ and Beak.

"Thataway, Jim!" shouted the Mohawk bench as every guy stood up and clapped. "Keep it going, Bernie! Another bingle!"

Bernie Drake, batting for Lee, bowed his head sadly as he turned away from the plate, a strikeout victim. Sam Suzuki waited out the pitches, then laced a belt-high, three-two pitch to deep left center, scoring Jim. He raced around the bases as if a bear were after him, and the coach held him up at third.

"He runs like a rabbit and hits farther

than any kid his size I've ever seen," said Dennis.

"How come he's got a new glove?" observed Daren Holden.

Stogie listened intently, wondering if Sam had told anyone else about his ruined glove.

"I don't know. He just says the old one's not good anymore and he wanted to get a new one."

Stogie swallowed and relaxed. Very few guys would keep a secret about a matter like that. You had to admit it — Sam was a great kid. *I don't know,* he thought. *In spite of what Sam thinks of me, I can't help but like him.*

Fuzzy flied out, ending the Mohawks' second three-run rally.

The Dukes failed to put a man on first in the top of the fifth. Dennis, leading off for the Mohawks, socked a high-bouncing grounder over Toots Martin's head for a single. Bob Sobus cut hard at a high pitch, but the ball skipped down toward third, was picked up by the third baseman and pegged to first. The throw was late. Dennis took advantage of the peg and raced to third.

Russ knocked a high fly to center field and Dennis, tagging up, bolted for home. "Hit the dirt, Den!" Beak shouted. "Hit it!"

Dennis hit it, but not in time. The relay from the outfield was almost perfect and Dennis was out by a yard. Beak popped up to first to end the fifth inning.

The Dukes got a man on first in the top of the sixth, but that's as far as he went. The Mohawks took the game, 7 to 6.

Stogie slid off the bench, thinking hard.

A couple of the guys were helping Coach Dirkus put the catching equipment and batting helmets into the canvas bag. Stogie walked up beside him.

"Coach," he said softly, "I'm sorry."

Coach Dirkus looked at him and grinned. "I figured you'd come around, Stogie. Sorry I didn't let you play, but I had to show you that the coach is still boss of his team."

Stogie nodded. "Yes, sir."

"See you at the next game, Stogie."

"Okay."

He started away when he saw a kid in uniform break away from a group of guys and come toward him. "Stogie," the kid called.

It was Sam Suzuki.

Stogie didn't know whether to wait for him or ignore him. He waited. "Yeah?"

"It was my fault you did not play. Right?"

Stogie's lips felt like cardboard. "Forget it," he said.

"Not easy to forget it," Sam replied.

"Well — try." Stogie started away, not knowing what else he could say.

"Stogie," Sam called quietly.

Stogie halted and looked directly into Sam's eyes. "Yeah, what?"

"Better I do not play anymore. Right? Better I quit."

Raw anger swept through Stogie in a wave. "No! It isn't better!" he shouted. "That would make everything worse! The guys would blame me for your quitting, just like you're blaming me for ruining your glove! And I didn't! You still think I did, don't you?"

Sam lifted his shoulders in a half-shrug. "I — I do not know, Stogie."

"What can I do to make you believe me?" Stogie cried. Then he turned and ran, catching up with Beak and Jill and his mother and father, who had already reached the sidewalk.

"What happened?" asked Jill wonderingly. "You didn't play at all."

Stogie swallowed and caught his breath. "I popped off to the coach."

"Popped off?" Jill's eyes turned big and round. "Why?"

"Because he wanted me to play second base. You saw Sam Suzuki at short, didn't you?"

"Yes, but —"

"Never mind, Jill," interrupted Mr. Crane. "Stogie will have to let that reprimanding cool off. I suspected it was some-thing like that when I saw Sam run out to short and Dennis to second." He paused. "Beak, you came through nicely."

"Thanks, Mr. Crane."

For a talkative guy Beak Peters was pretty quiet the rest of the way home. Guess even the hit wasn't enough to out-weigh the despair he shared with his pal Stogie.

# 9

BEAK came over the next afternoon. He handed Stogie a one-dollar bill and some change.

"That's from Sam Suzuki," explained Beak. "His share for breaking the Bunningers' window."

Stogie frowned. "You told him I paid for it?"

"I had to. He asked me."

A small volcano began to form in Stogie's stomach. Quickly he took the money inside and laid it on the dresser in his room. He took his time going back out to the porch.

"Sam told me he's going to New York City with his parents today," said Beak. "His father has some business to do there on Monday."

"Will they be back by Tuesday?"

The Mohawks were tangling with the Rainbows on Tuesday, and chances were good that Fats Cornell would hurl for the Rainbows. He was tough, one of the toughest in the league.

"I don't know," replied Beak. "I sure hope so. Without him we . . ." He broke off and looked sheepishly at Stogie. "He is pretty good, Stoge. You know that."

"Of course I know. And I know you were going to say that without him we might lose. Don't forget, we had a pretty good team before he came around, too."

"I know, Stoge. And I know he sure messed things up for you. But the guy's so *good*, you know it? I don't only mean as a ball player, but as a guy. He's a barrel of fun."

Stogie nodded. "Nobody said he's not a good guy. But don't you think he's pigheaded for still thinking I ruined his glove? I've never heard of anything so crazy!"

*Just the same,* he felt like saying, *I can't help being a little sore at Sam. It's his fault I'm not playing shortstop. His fault I'm playing second base where I won't get the action I got at short.*

Beak didn't answer. He stretched out his legs and began carving something in the soft dirt with the edge of his sneakers.

"I've got a tent," he said at last, breaking the long silence. "I've been thinking about putting it up tonight in the back-yard. Want to help me, and both of us spend the night in it?"

Stogie shrugged. "Sure." He was glad the subject had changed. He felt an ache in his stomach every time Sam Suzuki's name was mentioned.

His mother gave him permission to spend the night with Beak. Beak used a small hatchet to drive in the stakes while Stogie held up the tent. It was large enough for two sleeping bags and still had plenty of space in between.

They lay in their pajamas in the dark-ness, a chorus of crickets breaking the night's velvet silence. Beak said he wished they had a million dollars so that they could travel to Europe and see the Colos-seum, the Eiffel Tower, the Alps and a hundred other things. Then to Egypt to see the Sphinx and the pyramids, and to China to see the Great Wall. Man, it would be the coolest cool.

They kept talking and wishing, and suddenly a sound — a different sound from the chirping of the crickets — cut into the quiet night.

"What was that?" asked Stogie, quickly straining his ears.

"I don't know!" Beak whispered.

The sound continued. It was a grating noise and seemed to originate just outside of their tent.

"I'll take a look," whispered Stogie. He shoved aside the quilt blanket, pivoted off the bed, and peeked through the front of the tent. Nothing.

He held still for a moment. The noise had stopped. He started back for the cot when it started up again. He realized now that it was coming from the side. This time he went all the way out of the tent and around the corner. And stopped dead.

An animal about two feet long and shaped like an oversized football, except for a tail on one end and a snout on the other, seemed to swell up for a second. Stogie recognized it instantly. A porcupine!

"Beak!" he cried softly. "C'm here! Quick!"

Just then something bumped against him and he jumped. "I *am* here!" murmured Beak. "Hey, it . . . it's a porcupine!"

Even before Beak had the words out of his mouth, the animal was scurrying toward the woods beyond the yard.

"He was gnawing on something," observed Stogie. In the semidarkness he saw

the hatchet where Beak had left it after driving in the stakes. He picked it up, and instantly he knew.

"He was gnawing on this. The handle's all wet and rough."

Then he was staring after the porcupine which he could no longer see, and another thought struck him — struck him like the blow of a bat striking a ball.

"Beak! I've got it! That's what happened to Sam Suzuki's glove! It was the porcupine that chewed it up!"

"Stogie, you're right! It had to be!"

Stogie did an Indian war dance on the spot. "Boy, Beak, do I feel good! I won't be able to sleep a wink the rest of the night!"

He did though.

# IO

ON TUESDAY Stogie was itching to tell Sam about the porcupine so he could clear up the whole mess about the glove. But when he and Beak arrived at the Suzukis' house, no one was home.

"Guess I'll have to wait till tonight," he said. "I'll see him at the game. I hope he'll be there."

They were at the ball park at 5:15 when most of the guys came drifting in. They played catch, then had batting practice, hitting three and laying one down. Sam Suzuki still hadn't shown up.

*In a way*, thought Stogie, *I don't care if Sam never shows up. Then I can go back to my old position at short.* But Stogie knew he didn't really mean it. He had to tell Sam what he had discovered about the glove.

Maybe — a thought brought a gleam into his eyes — maybe the coach would let him play short while Sam was gone!

"Anybody know where Sam Suzuki is?" inquired Coach Dirkus.

"In New York City with his parents," answered Beak.

"When are they coming back?"

"I don't know."

The coach picked up a bat and a ball. "Okay, let's have infield," he announced. "Dennis, take short, Stogie, second."

Stogie's hope collapsed like a punctured tire. He had thought sure . . . Lips pressed tightly together, he picked up his mitt and ran out to second. He wasn't going to argue with the coach again. No fun warming the bench.

The coach rapped out grounders for ten minutes, then the Rainbows took over the field. At 6:30, game time, Sam Suzuki still hadn't appeared.

The Rainbows had first raps. Tom Rolf, pitching for the Mohawks, walked the lead-off man. The second man blasted a hot grounder directly at Stogie. Stogie stooped to snare it — it looked like a soft catch — but the ball zipped past his glove, through his legs, and to the outfield!

"Get your tail down, Stogie!" yelled a fan.

Playing second base wasn't as easy as he had thought!

Stogie rushed back, caught the throw-in

from right fielder Bernie Drake, and held it. The man on first had advanced to third, and the hitter was standing comfortably on first.

"Sorry, Tom," said Stogie, tossing the ball to the pitcher. Tom's tightened lips showed that he wasn't at all happy with that play.

Tom winged in two outside pitches on the next hitter, then struck him out. A Texas leaguer over short scored a run. Jim Albanese pulled in a fly for the second out, and Bob Sobus caught a pop fly for the third.

"Wish Sam would show up," said Fuzzy in the dugout, tapping his bat against the tips of his sneakers. "He's smaller than most of us, but he's good."

Daren Holden grinned at Stogie. "You don't think so, though, do you, Stoge?"

Stogie shrugged. "Who says I don't? Sure, he's good."

"But you don't like him. You don't like his taking over your favorite position."

Stogie's control shattered like glass. "You'd better close your trap and keep it closed, Holden!"

Daren chuckled and Stogie, his face still burning, turned his attention to Jim Albanese standing at the plate. He wished more than ever that Sam would return. *I hope that when I tell him what I saw he'll forget about the ruined glove and be my friend,* Stogie thought. *I really want him to be my friend.*

Fats Cornell couldn't get one over and Jim Albanese got a free ticket to first. Lee Cragg, up next, laid down a nice bunt between third base and the pitcher, advancing Jim. Fats threw Lee out at first.

Dennis Krupa fouled the first two pitches, then blasted a high fly to left. The Rainbow left fielder caught it. Fuzzy Caliel went after a high pitch for strike one, then slammed a low one in a crazy, sizzling grounder to Fats. Fats dropped to his knees, trapped the ball between his fat legs, and threw Fuzzy out.

Three away. No runs, no hits, no errors.

And still no Sam.

# 11

THE RAINBOW lead-off hitter socked a belt-high pitch directly back at Tom Rolf. Tom caught it and stared at the ball in the pocket of his glove as if he were surprised he had it. He tossed it to first and the ball zipped around the horn.

"Two more, Tom!" Bob Sobus hollered. "Let's get two more!"

The second Rainbow hitter blasted Tom's first pitch to right center for two bases. Then a grass-cutting grounder zipped down to short. Dennis fielded it and threw it wild to first. A run scored and the hitter trotted to second.

Stogie kicked a pebble, then picked it up and threw it beyond the foul line. It was only the top of the second inning and he could already foresee the end of the ball game. The Rainbows were going to smear the Mohawks but good.

The next batter socked a high-bouncing grounder to third. Fuzzy snared it and whipped it to first. Out! Bob Sobus shifted his position to peg to third, but the runner stayed glued on second.

A hard blow over Tom's head scored the Rainbows' second run. He struck out the next man to retire the side. Rainbows 3, Mohawks 0.

"Start it off, Stogie," encouraged Coach Dirkus. "Get a hit."

Fats Cornell wound up and breezed a

pitch past Stogie's ear. Stogie reared back. "Ball!" yelled the ump.

Fats's second pitch cut the outside corner. "Steeerike!"

Fats's third started to cut the center of the plate and Stogie swung. *Crack!* The ball zoomed out to left center. Stogie lost his helmet as he rounded first. The helmet bounced on the base path and stopped near the grass about the same time that Stogie stopped at second base.

Time was called and Stogie got his helmet.

Bob Sobus, after fouling two pitches, grounded out to short. Bernie went the limit, three balls and two strikes, then struck out. The Rainbows chattered like crazy and Stogie wondered if he'd die on second.

Tony Francis blasted the first pitch

through short and the coach at third wind-milled Stogie in. The Rainbow shortstop took the throw-in from left and pegged it in to home, but Stogie was already there. Tony advanced to second on the play.

Tom Rolf stepped to the plate and waited out Fats Cornell's pitches to a two-and-two count. Then he popped one high to first base for the third out.

"Well, we've broken the ice, anyway," said the coach. "Now go and get 'em out."

The Rainbow lead-off man singled on the first pitch. The next drove a hot grounder to second. Stogie crouched to pick it up and missed the hop. The ball struck his left knee and glanced behind first. Bob Sobus hightailed after it, picked it up and hurled it to third to get the first runner heading there from second. The

throw was too high! The runner rounded third and scored, and the second runner stopped on second base.

*Nice!* Stogie muttered to himself. *Sobus and I are both playing a nice game — for the Rainbows!*

The Rainbows didn't stop there. They scored twice more before the Mohawks could get them out. At the end of the top of the third inning the scoreboard read, Rainbows 6, Mohawks 1.

"They're burying us," said Fuzzy as he plunked himself on the bench. "We're just not playing baseball."

"Get hold of yourselves," Coach Dirkus said firmly to the team. "Keep loose out there and keep your heads up. You're not thinking. Think ahead every minute. Say to yourself, 'What'll I do if the ball's hit to me?' Have that answer in your head and you won't get mixed up when the ball does come to you. The old fight, now. Let's go!"

If Jim Albanese had any of the old fight in him before, he didn't have it now. He popped the second pitch to short. Lee Cragg put some life into the team with a single through short, but Dennis struck out and Fuzzy grounded out to second.

"I hardly got to sit down!" grunted Bernie, running across the diamond with Stogie.

"I'm up first next inning," said Stogie. "It'll be the second time."

"Better do something!" Bernie said. "My father says a game's never over till the last inning."

"Is he here?"

"Try to keep him away! But this is one game that's over already."

The first Rainbow drove Tom's first pitch through the hole between third and short, and it seemed as if the Rainbows were rolling again. A pop-up to Fuzzy Caliel, and then a fly to center fielder Daren Holden, who had taken Lee Cragg's place, brightened the Mohawks' hopes. Then Tom, after throwing a wide pitch to the batter, winged three strikes over the plate. The batter swung at the last one and missed it a foot. Three away.

Stogie ran in, looking for Sam. But Sam still hadn't shown up.

"Start it off again, Stoge!" yelled a fan.

"Sharpen up your tomahawks, you Mohawk Indians, and get some hits, will you?" cried another.

Stogie pulled on his helmet, selected his favorite bat, and stepped to the plate. Fats drilled a strike past him, then drilled in another. Stogie swung. "Strike two!" cried the ump.

Fats threw a bad one, then came in with a pitch that looked slightly inside. Stogie couldn't take the chance of being called out. He cut at it. *Crack!* A line drive between short and third for a neat single!

"Thataway to go, Stoge!" screamed the fans.

Bob followed up with a single too, and Stogie raced around to third. Beak Peters, batting for Bernie, socked a grounder to short. The Mohawk fans groaned as the ball zipped to second and then to first for a double play. Stogie stayed on third, playing it safe. Tony rapped a grounder to second which sizzled through the player's legs, and Stogie scored.

Tom walked and Russ Russo, pinch-hitting for Jim Albanese, stepped to the plate. He waited out Fats Cornell's pitches, got a two-and-two count, then laced the next pitch to short left. The left fielder came running in hard, but didn't seem to be covering the ground fast enough.

He did though. He caught the ball one-handed and received a whopping cheer from the Rainbow fans. Rainbows 6, Mohawks 2.

Two innings to go. It was possible for the Mohawks to beat the Rainbows, but not probable. Not probable at all. It was too much to expect.

Stogie reached his position at second.

When he turned, his eyes popped. There, around the corner of the stands, came Sam, running as hard as he could!

"Hey, look who's here!" he shouted. "It's Sam!"

# 12

COACH DIRKUS sent Sam immediately out to short in place of Dennis. Sam's face sparkled with a broad grin. "Hi, Fuzzy! Hi, Stogie!" He waved to the guys in the outfield, who shouted, "Hi, Sam!"

*Look at the greeting he's getting,* thought Stogie. *The guys really like him. Guess I'm the only one . . . Heck! I like him, too! It's just that I don't like his taking over shortstop from me. He didn't really take it. Coach Dirkus put him there*

108

*for his own reasons. I'll never get over that part of it. I don't think I will, anyway.*

"Got something to tell you after the game, Sam!" he cried. "Something about your glove!"

The sparkle on Sam's face diminished a little. "What is something?"

"You'll see!"

"Steeerike!" shouted the ump as Tom grooved the first pitch to the Rainbow lead-off hitter.

"Where've you been?" asked Fuzzy. "The game's almost over!"

"Impossible to leave early from New York City!" Sam replied. "I keep telling my father, 'Hurry! Hurry! Hurry! I must play baseball!' He says he is hurrying!" Sam shrugged. "Lucky to be here now!"

"Yes, but it's probably too late," replied Fuzzy dismally.

*Crack!* A hard grounder to Stogie's right side. He rushed over, fielded the hop and snapped the ball to first. Out!

"Nice play, Stogie!" yelled Sam.

Stogie grinned. Who else would praise you on a play while still thinking you were responsible for ruining a glove autographed by one of Japan's greatest baseball players? Who else would play with you as if nothing had happened, though you knew that he was still hurt. Sam really believed that Stogie had ruined his glove. Some guys might hate you for it, might want you to pay for the glove. Not Sam. He had wanted nothing.

A high pop-up over the pitcher's box. "I'll take it!" Tom shouted.

He took it. Two away.

The third Rainbow came up. Tom grooved a pitch for strike one. His second pitch was slightly higher. The batter swung. *Crack!* A solid blow! The ball shot to deep left. It kept going . . . going . . . and dropped over the fence for a home run!

*We're licked,* thought Stogie gloomily. *The Rainbows are ahead of us, 7 to 2, and we have only two more raps.* It was hopeless.

Tom struck out the next Rainbow and the Mohawks came to bat. Daren Holden led off. Fats couldn't get more than one strike over the plate and Daren got a free pass to first. Sam Suzuki was up next.

"Your meat, Sam!" Beak yelled. The fans gave Sam a big hand too.

Sam took a called strike, then two balls. Fats wiped his sweating face, stepped on the mound and delivered. Smack! A bullet drive in the hole between left and center!

The ball dropped between the outfielders and kept rolling. Daren scored and Sam held up at third.

The Mohawk bench was wild with excitement. "Keep it going, Fuzz! Bring 'im in!"

Fuzzy didn't. He grounded out to short. Stogie strode to the plate. He felt great.

The pitch. Stogie swung. A ground ball through short! Sam scored and Stogie stood on first for his third hit of the game. Bob flied out to left and Beak stepped into the box, his bat under his armpit while he jiggled the helmet firmly on his head.

Fats got two balls on him, then a strike, then threw two more balls. Beak walked.

Two outs, two men on, and Tony Francis was up. No one had much faith in Tony's hitting. He had knocked a single the first time up, and got on base by virtue

of an error the second time. His luck couldn't last.

But it did. He singled to right, scoring Stogie, and Beak raced around to third. Tom Rolf singled, too, but it was a scratch hit, a slow dribbler down to third that advanced Tony to second.

Russ Russo ended the big inning by grounding out to short. Rainbows 7, Mohawks 5.

The top of the sixth. Each Mohawk was alive with spark and noise. He was going to make sure no ball would go by him.

A smashing drive to short! Sam Suzuki got in front of it, fielded it neatly, pegged it to first. One away!

A poke over first base! It looked certain to be a hit. Bob ran back . . . back . . . and caught the ball over his shoulder! Two away!

"One more to get, Tom! One more!"

A high smash to deep center! Daren stood a moment, not moving, as if he had lost sight of the ball. And then he stepped back, raised his glove, and the white pill dropped into it.

"Man, Daren!" Stogie cried as he waited for the center fielder to come running in. "Thought you had misjudged that one for sure."

"I did!" said Daren, laughing.

This was it. The last of the sixth. The Mohawks' last chance. Daren was first man up. Sam, Fuzzy and Stogie would follow. Fats drilled a strike down the heart of the plate, then another. Daren sent the third pitch out to center, where it was caught for out number one.

Coach Dirkus strode in front of the bench, clapping his hands. "Some life, men! Talk it up! Don't sink into the dumps now!"

They talked it up. "Blast it outa the park, Sam! You did it before, do it again! He's the same pitcher!"

*Crack!* A line drive over Fats Cornell's head and Sam stood on first for a single, his second hit.

Fuzzy went the limit, three balls and two strikes, then struck out.

"Keep it alive, Stogie!" yelled a fan. "Blast it!"

Stogie waited for a good one. It came in. He cut hard and met the ball solidly. The hit was a clothesline drive over the third baseman's head that went for a triple, scoring Sam.

"Are you going to pay Fats after the game, Stoge?" asked Jim, who was coaching third. "That was your fourth hit."

"Pay, my eye." Stogie grinned.

Bob walked. Beak socked a double, scoring Stogie. The ball game was tied up! The Mohawk bench jumped and yelled. The Mohawk fans went almost delirious. The winning run was on third. But the bottom of the batting order was up. The poorest hitters.

Tony waited out the pitches and got a walk! Fats, sweat glistening on his brow, drilled two pitches over the plate on Tom, and it looked as if the game would go into an extra inning. Then, *crack!* A blow over second! Bob scored! It was over! The Mohawks had done the impossible. They had come from far behind and won, 8 to 7.

# 13

"YOU CAME just in time, Sam!" cried Stogie. "If it weren't for you we would've lost for sure!"

Sam was grinning. "You did okay yourself! Four hits! Oh, man!"

After the shouting died down and the crowd was moving out of the park, Stogie motioned to Sam. "Come here, Sam. I told you I had something to tell you about your old glove."

Stogie was with his mother and father and Jill. They all congratulated Sam on his playing. Beak came running up, too.

"What do you have to tell me?" asked Sam, his eyes flitting from one face to another.

Stogie's eyes were dancing. "Beak and I, we know what it was that ruined your glove. And it wasn't me, Sam. I kept telling you it wasn't."

Sam blinked his eyes. He moved his gloved hand behind him. "Who do you think ruined my glove, Stogie?"

"A porcupine."

"*Porcupine?*" Sam's brows knitted.

"Yes. Beak and I saw one the other night while we were camping out in his backyard. We heard a noise, something gnawing on wood, so we crawled out of the tent and saw this animal chewing on Beak's hatchet. The handle. It stayed long

**119**

enough for us to see it and then took off as if its tail was on fire."

A warm glow started over Sam's face. "Porcupine, huh? Funny name, porcupine."

"We'll show you a picture of it sometime," said Beak, smiling.

The glow seemed to fade. Was there still doubt in Sam's mind? And then Stogie remembered that he hadn't explained everything to Sam.

"Porcupines like salt," he said. "They'll chew up anything that has salt on it. Your glove did. And so did the handle of Beak's hatchet. You've just got to see that hatchet, Sam. You won't believe it."

The glow returned, and Sam's eyes brightened.

"I will believe it, Stogie," he said seriously. "And I believe you. I really do. I just hope you are not mad at me anymore for stealing your position at shortstop."

Stogie grinned. "I'm not, Sam. And I mean it, too."

# How many of these Matt Christopher sports classics have you read?

## Baseball
❒ Baseball Pals
❒ Catcher with a Glass Arm
❒ The Diamond Champs
❒ The Fox Steals Home
❒ The Kid Who Only Hit Homers
❒ Look Who's Playing First Base
❒ Miracle at the Plate
❒ No Arm in Left Field
❒ Shortstop from Tokyo
❒ The Year Mom Won the Pennant

## Basketball
❒ Johnny Long Legs
❒ Long Shot for Paul

## Dirt Bike Racing
❒ Dirt Bike Racer
❒ Dirt Bike Runaway

## Football
❒ Catch That Pass!
❒ The Counterfeit Tackle
❒ Football Fugitive
❒ Tight End
❒ Touchdown for Tommy
❒ Tough to Tackle

## Ice Hockey
❒ Face-Off
❒ Ice Magic

## Soccer
❒ Soccer Halfback

## Track
❒ Run, Billy, Run

All available in paperback from Little, Brown and Company

---

# Join the Matt Christopher Fan Club!

To become an official member of the Matt Christopher Fan Club, send a self-addressed, stamped envelope (#10, business-letter size) to:

Matt Christopher Fan Club
34 Beacon Street
Boston, MA 02108